YOU ARE OH SO HORRIBLY HANDSOME!

Eva Dax and Sabine Dully

STARFISH BAY
CHILDREN'S BOOKS

This is Gregor,
a little monster.

grrOaaar

He could shout ear-splittingly loud.
No doubt about that.

Gregor was horrendously strong.
That was a fact.

And he could run frighteningly fast.
Nobody would question that, either.

But one day,
    Gregor had a nasty thought.

He looked at his big nose
    and his sticking-out ears,
    and he asked himself,
      "Am I handsome?"

He went to see his mommy.
"Am I handsome?" he asked.

"Of course you are," said Mommy.
"I don't know anyone
who can **squint** as handsomely as you!"

And she kissed and cuddled Gregor.

Then Gregor asked his daddy,
"Am I handsome?"

"You certainly are!" said Daddy.
"You've got the **stinkiest, cheesiest** feet **in the whole world!**"

And he threw his little son high in the air.

Then Gregor asked his granddad, "Am I handsome?"

"You are the handsomest grandson I ever saw!" said Granddad, puffing hard on his pipe. "Nobody else has teeth as **rotten, crooked, and yellow** as yours!"

And he took Gregor on his lap
and put his big, strong arms round him.

Loch Ness

Then Gregor asked his old neighbor,
  "Am I handsome?"

"No doubt about it!" she croaked.
"Your face is full of the biggest,
bumpiest, muckiest, yuckiest
warts I ever did see!"

And she lovingly pinched
his cheek.

Giftig!!!

Then Gregor asked his little brother, "Am I handsome?"

"You bet!" said his brother. "You've got the fattest, flabbiest, softest, squashiest, wibbly-wobbliest tummy I know!"

And he put his little arms round Gregor's big belly.

Next Gregor asked his best friend.
"Am I handsome?"

"Absolutely!" she said.
"You've got the **roughest, toughest, greyest, greasiest, scaliest, scabbiest** skin that any monster ever had!"

And she gave Gregor a sloppy kiss on the nose.

Gregor looked in the mirror again.
He gazed at his big nose, his sticking-out ears,
and his squinting eyes.

His **stinky, cheesy** feet.
His **rotten, crooked, yellow** teeth.

His **big, bumpy, mucky, yucky** warts.

His **fat, flabby, soft, squashy,
wibbly-wobbly** tummy.

And his **rough, tough, grey,
greasy, scaly, scabby skin.**

Then he thought about how his mummy
had kissed and cuddled him.

How his daddy had thrown him in the air,
and his granddad had taken him onto his lap.

How his neighbor had lovingly pinched his cheek,
his brother had put his arms round his tummy,
and his best friend had given him a kiss on the nose.
And now—all of a sudden—he could see it, too:

It was true. He really was handsome!

www.starfishbaypublishing.com

YOU ARE OH SO HORRIBLY HANDSOME!

First North American edition Published by Starfish Bay Children's Books in 2016
978-1-76036-029-0
Du bist so schrecklich schön! © Verlag Friedrich Oetinger, Hamburg 2015.
Published by agreement with Verlag Friedrich Oetinger.
Translated by David-Henry Wilson
Printed and bound in China by Beijing Shangtang Print & Packaging Co., Ltd
11 Tengren Road, Niulanshan Town, Shunyi District, Beijing, China

Eva Dax studied literary science and journalism and worked for radio and television before becoming what she is today, a consultant and editor at SWR radio in Germany.

Sabine Dully has a degree in communication design and has been working in children's television for several years in Germany.